A Gift for the King

A Persian Tale · Retold and illustrated by

Christopher Manson

Henry Holt and Company · New York

Once there was a king named Artaxerxes who ruled a great empire.

He was very rich. He had many servants and brave soldiers who obeyed his every order. He lived in a marvelous colored palace filled with beautiful things.

It was a law of the land that all who came to visit the king were required to bring him a gift. Over the years the king had received many wonderful presents. Every day people from all the different lands of the empire brought King Artaxerxes beautiful and costly things.

The king's treasury was full of gold and silver. The king's palace was full of objects made of ivory and precious stones, furniture made of cedar and ebony wood, gorgeous clothes, golden cups and alabaster bowls.

But the day came when the king took no pleasure in all this.

So King Artaxerxes jumped up and, without a word, went walking, not knowing where he was going.

He walked through his beautiful colored palace, through the carved and painted halls and shining courtyards, and out the door.

The king had never walked anywhere before. He was always carried by his servants or driven along in one of his gilded chariots. Everyone was astonished.

The king's attendants hurried after him, wondering where he was going.

Outside the palace King Artaxerxes met two merchants. They said, "O great king! May you live a hundred years! We have gifts for you—rare incense and sweet perfumes from all over the world!" And they showed the king what they had brought to him. Each jar contained a rich, rare and costly scent.

The king shrugged his shoulders and said to his attendants, "When we return, put the perfumes and incense with all the rest of my perfumes and incense."

Then he walked on.

Beyond the palace gardens King Artaxerxes met a nobleman who ordered his servants to display beautiful robes as the king walked by.

"O great king!" said the nobleman. "May you live a thousand years! I have brought you robes of fine wool and silk woven through with gold and silver threads. Please accept this gift from your most loyal subject."

The king signaled his attendants to take up the present and said with a sigh, "When we return to the palace, put these robes with all my other robes."

Then he walked on.

Coming down from the hills, King Artaxerxes met one of his generals marching along with an army of brave soldiers.

The general had his trumpeters sound a salute to the king. Then he said, "O great king! May you live ten thousand years! It is my great honor to present you with this golden bow, this golden quiver full of golden arrows and this great golden shield. May these presents serve you and protect you always!"

The king waved his staff and said to his attendants, "Bring these things along, and when we return to the palace, put them in the armory with all my other arms."

Then he walked on.

Out on the plains King Artaxerxes walked by the tower where the royal stargazers lived. They happened to look down, and when they saw the king, they ran out of their tower to meet him.

"O great king!" they said. "May you live a hundred thousand years! We have made a statue in your likeness that will show your strength and majesty for all time! We hope this present pleases you."

The king looked over the statue glittering with silver and colored stones and said to his attendants, "When we return to the palace, put the statue in the room with all my other statues."

Then he walked on.

In the desert King Artaxerxes met a caravan of traders from distant lands who threw themselves down before him and said, "O great king! May you live a million years! We have traveled for many weeks to bring you these strong camels loaded with rugs woven of the finest, softest wool to be found any-where! We hope you will enjoy our gift."

The king said to his attendants, "When we return, put the camels in my stables with all my other camels and throw the rugs on the floor."

Then he walked on.

Finally King Artaxerxes met ambassadors from a neighboring kingdom bringing many rich presents as tribute.

"O great king!" said one ambassador. "May you live *forever*! See what we have brought you: a chariot with swift little horses; three singing ladies who will sing songs about your greatness; bronze vessels full of gold and silver; golden bowls; vases and cups of alabaster; pearls and gems; and caskets of jewels, bracelets, earrings and necklaces! Our only hope is that you will find these things pleasing!"

The king looked wearily at all the gifts and told his attendants, "When we return, put all these gifts with all my other gifts in the palace."

Then the king sat down to rest.

For some reason King Artaxerxes took no pleasure in all his presents.

His faithful attendant said, "O great king! You are surely the richest king who has ever lived. Your treasuries are heaped high with gold and silver; your palace is enriched with every precious gift to be found in the world. Just look at these jewels shining in the sun! What more could you want?"

"I have never walked so far before. My throat is dry as a desert stone!" The king thought for a moment and said, "I want a cool drink."

Of course, anything the king said had the force of law, and anything the king wanted, he must have.

So everyone looked through all the wonderful gifts to find something for the king to drink.

They searched the baskets and caskets, the bags and the bundles. They looked in the vases and vessels, the jugs and the jars. In desperation they even looked over the camels and the carpets and the coins and the coffers.

But there was nothing for the king to drink.

"Where is my drink?" demanded the king.

His attendants threw themselves down in the dust before him.

"O great king!" they said. "There is nothing to drink! The bottles are filled with perfume, and the cups are filled with pearls."

"By the great shining sun!" cried the angry king. "I have never been so thirsty before!"

Just then a poor shepherd boy happened to come along, and he said, "O great king, I am only a poor shepherd. If we were back in the hills where I live, I would give you my fattest sheep and the sweetest milk of my flock. But here I have only this old water jar. I hope you are not displeased."

King Artaxerxes lifted up the old jar, which was cool to the touch. The sound of water splashing inside was the sweetest music he had ever heard.

He poured some water into a bowl, where it glistened and glittered like a heap of diamonds.

He lifted the bowl of precious liquid to his lips and took a deep, deep drink.

The king had never tasted anything so good.

The jar of water pleased the king more than any gift he had been given all that day.

He was so pleased that he gave the horses, the chariot and the camels to the ambassador and told him to ride home with the singing ladies.

Then the king turned to the boy and said, "Because your gift has pleased me so much, I give you all these gifts in exchange."

And so it was done.

Then great King Artaxerxes, ruler of a rich and powerful empire, walked happily home, carrying his favorite gift.

When the king arrived at his palace, he was so happy, no one knew what had happened. They all thought the old jar must be full of something unbelievably precious.

And, of course, they were right.

A Note About the Book

This story is based on a tale from *The Palace of Pleasure*, a collection by William Painter published in 1566. Painter found the tale in the works of a third-century Roman writer named Aelian.

Artaxerxes was the king of Persia from 464 to 424 B.C.; he ruled an empire that stretched from Greece to India. Many countries paid tribute to the empire, and the Persians became known for their fabulous wealth and luxurious living. It is recorded that when Alexander the Great finally captured Persepolis, the chief city of Persia, in 330 B.C., it took three thousand camels and innumerable mules to carry away the treasure.

The kings of Persia were absolute monarchs. Everyone was required to obey their orders, and their word was law. They never walked outside their palaces, but were carried everywhere. They maintained lavish courts and entertained thousands of guests every day.

The Persians employed artists and craftsmen from many lands to build and decorate their exquisite palaces. The art of Babylonia, Assyria, Greece, and Egypt influenced the art of Persia.

The wealth and glory of the Persian kings are long gone, but the stately processions of guards and tribute bearers carved on their palace walls still march up flights of crumbling stairs to empty throne rooms. I have used these carvings, as well as historical reconstructions of costumes, furniture, and buildings, as sources for my pictures.

C.M.

1917

For Matthew

Copyright © 1989 by Christopher Manson

All rights reserved, including the right to reproduce this book or portions thereof in any form.

Published by Henry Holt and Company, Inc., 115 West 18th Street, New York, New York 10011.

Published in Canada by Fitzhenry & Whiteside Limited, 195 Allstate Parkway, Markham, Ontario L3R 4T8.

Library of Congress Cataloging in Publication Data

Manson, Christopher.   A gift for the king : a Persian tale / retold and illustrated by Christopher Manson. — 1st ed.   p.   cm.

Based on a tale from The palace of pleasure by William Painter published in 1566.

Summary: King Artaxerxes is not satisfied by any of the gifts he receives until a shepherd boy gives him a plain jar of water.   ISBN 0-8050-0951-5

[1. Folklore—Iran.]   I. Painter, William, 1540?–1594. Palace of pleasure. II. Title. PZ8.1.M2985Gi 1989 398.2'2'0955—dc19 [E]   88-28430

Henry Holt books are available at special discounts for bulk purchases for sales promotions, premiums,
fund-raising, or educational use. Special editions or book excerpts can also be created to specification.
For details, contact: Special Sales Director, Henry Holt & Co., Inc., 115 West 18th Street, New York, New York 10011.

First edition │ Designed by Marc Cheshire │ Printed in Hong Kong
1 3 5 7 9 10 8 6 4 2